Time Pieces

for
Horn

Music through the Ages in Two Volumes
for Horn in F or E flat

Volume 1

Paul Harris and Andrew Skirrow

ABRSM

CONTENTS

Time Pieces for Horn

Volume 1

*c.***1500**   # Fortune, lesse moy

Anon.

Published by ABRSM (Publishing) Ltd, a wholly owned subsidiary of ABRSM

AB 2841

c.1500   A Galyard

Anon.

The galliard, or 'galyard' as it was known in England, was a lively 16th-century court dance. The music was nearly always in triple metre, and often included the 'hemiola': two bars of triple time sounding as if they were three units of two. Can you find instances of this here?

1597 The Frog Galliard

John Dowland
(1563–1626)

The original *Frog Galliard* is for solo lute, although a song by Dowland, 'Now, O now I needs must part' (1597), uses this same melody. See the footnote above for an explanation of a 'galliard'.

1601 When Laura Smiles
from *A Booke of Ayres*

Philip Rosseter
(1567/8–1623)

1612 The Earl of Salisbury's Pavan

William Byrd
(*c*.1540–1623)

Another 16th-century court dance, the 'pavan' (It. *pavana*; Fr. *pavane*) is a slow, processional kind of dance. Most pavans are in simple quadruple time and tend to precede the faster dances, notably the galliard.

1746 See, the Conqu'ring Hero Comes

from *Judas Maccabaeus*

George Frideric Handel
(1685–1759)

c.1760 German Dance

Hob. IX/22 No. 7

Joseph Haydn
(1732–1809)

'German Dance' was a generic term for couple-dances in triple metre. The most popular of these were the waltz and the *ländler* (a slow waltz).

1788 Nel cor più non mi sento

from *L'amor contrastato*

Giovanni Paisiello
(1740–1816)

Translated, this title is 'My heart no longer feels'. A duet from the Italian opera *L'amor contrastato* (also known as *La molinara*), this popular piece was the basis for variations by several composers, including Beethoven, J. N. Hummel and N. Paganini.

1821 Theme from *Der Freischütz* Overture

Carl Maria von Weber
(1786–1826)

AB 2841

1848 Soldiers' March

from *Album for the Young*, Op. 68

Robert Schumann
(1810–1856)

Horn in F

Piano

Allegro deciso ♩ = *c.*120

1873 St Anthony Chorale

Johannes Brahms
(1833–1897)

from *Variations on a Theme by Haydn*, Op. 56a

Andante ♩ = 72

Horn in F

Piano

AB 2841

Time Pieces for Horn

Horn in E♭

Volume 1

*c.*1500   Fortune, lesse moy

Anon.

*c.*1500   A Galyard

Anon.

The galliard, or 'galyard' as it was known in England, was a lively 16th-century court dance. The music was nearly always in triple metre, and often included the 'hemiola': two bars of triple time sounding as if they were three units of two. Can you find instances of this here?

AB 2841

1597   The Frog Galliard

John Dowland
(1563–1626)

The original *Frog Galliard* is for solo lute, although a song by Dowland, 'Now, O now I needs must part' (1597), uses this same melody. See the footnote above for an explanation of a 'galliard'.

1601   When Laura Smiles

from *A Booke of Ayres*

Philip Rosseter
(1567/8–1623)

1612   The Earl of Salisbury's Pavan

William Byrd
(c.1540–1623)

Another 16th-century court dance, the 'pavan' (It. *pavana*; Fr. *pavane*) is a slow, processional kind of dance. Most pavans are in simple quadruple time and tend to precede the faster dances, notably the galliard.

1746 See, the Conqu'ring Hero Comes

from *Judas Maccabaeus*

George Frideric Handel
(1685–1759)

*c.*1760 German Dance

Hob. IX/22 No. 7

Joseph Haydn
(1732–1809)

'German Dance' was a generic term for couple-dances in triple metre. The most popular of these were the waltz and the *ländler* (a slow waltz).

1788 Nel cor più non mi sento

from *L'amor contrastato*

Giovanni Paisiello
(1740–1816)

Translated, this title is 'My heart no longer feels'. A duet from the Italian opera *L'amor contrastato* (also known as *La molinara*), this popular piece was the basis for variations by several composers, including Beethoven, J. N. Hummel and N. Paganini.

1821 Theme from *Der Freischütz* Overture

Carl Maria von Weber
(1786–1826)

Adagio ♩ = *c*.60

1848 Soldiers' March

from *Album for the Young*, Op. 68

Robert Schumann
(1810–1856)

Allegro deciso ♩ = *c*.120

1873 St Anthony Chorale

from *Variations on a Theme by Haydn*, Op. 56a

Johannes Brahms
(1833–1897)

The 'St Anthony' Variations by Brahms was based on a chorale attributed to Joseph Haydn. In fact the original chorale, scored for wind instruments, is probably not the work of Haydn.

1881 Agnus Dei

from *Messe basse*

Gabriel Fauré
(1845–1924)

AB 2841

1886 **Wine Cellar**

from *50 Russian Folksongs*

Pyotr Il'yich Tchaikovsky
(1840–1893)

1896 O Mistress Mine
from *The Clown's Songs from 'Twelfth Night'*, Op. 65

Sir Charles Villiers Stanford
(1852–1924)

1908/9 No. 3 from *For Children*, Vol. 1

Béla Bartók
(1881–1945)

A collection of piano pieces, *For Children* was inspired by Slovakian or, as in this case, Hungarian folk music, which Bartók collected and recorded from 1906 onwards.

1923 Lullaby
from *Five Piano Pieces*

Frederick Delius
(1862–1934)

(The original metronome marking, for the piano piece, is ♩ = 44–48.)

1940 Song at Dusk
from *Duets for Children*

William Walton
(1902–1983)

Larghetto ♩ = 69

p espressivo

1940 Trumpet Tune
from *Duets for Children*

William Walton
(1902–1983)

Alla marcia ♩ = 144

AB 2841

Time Pieces for Horn

Horn in F

Volume 1

*c.*1500 Fortune, lesse moy

Anon.

*c.*1500 A Galyard

Anon.

The galliard, or 'galyard' as it was known in England, was a lively 16th-century court dance. The music was nearly always in triple metre, and often included the 'hemiola': two bars of triple time sounding as if they were three units of two. Can you find instances of this here?

AB 2841

1597 The Frog Galliard

John Dowland
(1563–1626)

The original *Frog Galliard* is for solo lute, although a song by Dowland, 'Now, O now I needs must part' (1597), uses this same melody. See the footnote above for an explanation of a 'galliard'.

1601 When Laura Smiles

from *A Booke of Ayres*

Philip Rosseter
(1567/8–1623)

1612 The Earl of Salisbury's Pavan

William Byrd
(c.1540–1623)

Another 16th-century court dance, the 'pavan' (It. *pavana*; Fr. *pavane*) is a slow, processional kind of dance. Most pavans are in simple quadruple time and tend to precede the faster dances, notably the galliard.

1746 See, the Conqu'ring Hero Comes

from *Judas Maccabaeus*

George Frideric Handel
(1685–1759)

*c.*1760 German Dance

Hob. IX/22 No. 7

Joseph Haydn
(1732–1809)

'German Dance' was a generic term for couple-dances in triple metre. The most popular of these were the waltz and the *ländler* (a slow waltz).

1788 Nel cor più non mi sento

from *L'amor contrastato*

Giovanni Paisiello
(1740–1816)

Translated, this title is 'My heart no longer feels'. A duet from the Italian opera *L'amor contrastato* (also known as *La molinara*), this popular piece was the basis for variations by several composers, including Beethoven, J. N. Hummel and N. Paganini.

AB 2841

1821 # Theme from
Der Freischütz **Overture**

Carl Maria von Weber
(1786–1826)

1848 # Soldiers' March
from *Album for the Young*, Op. 68

Robert Schumann
(1810–1856)

1873 St Anthony Chorale

from *Variations on a Theme by Haydn*, Op. 56a

Johannes Brahms
(1833–1897)

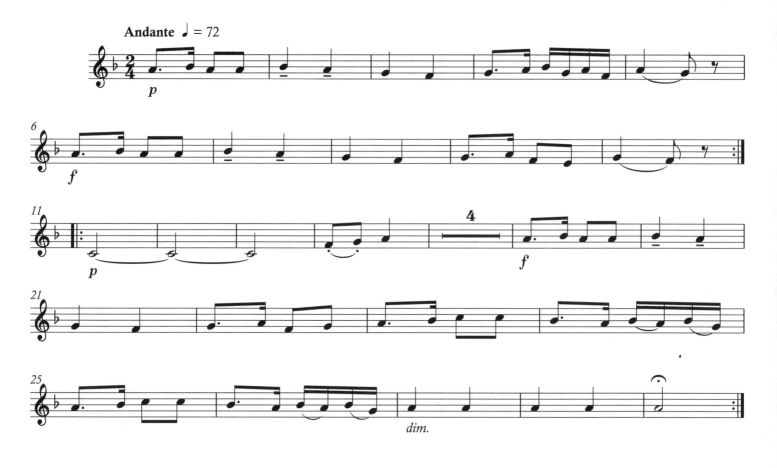

The 'St Anthony' Variations by Brahms was based on a chorale attributed to Joseph Haydn. In fact the original chorale, scored for wind instruments, is probably not the work of Haydn.

1881 Agnus Dei

from *Messe basse*

Gabriel Fauré
(1845–1924)

1886 Wine Cellar
from *50 Russian Folksongs*

Pyotr Il'yich Tchaikovsky
(1840–1893)

1896 O Mistress Mine

from *The Clown's Songs from 'Twelfth Night'*, Op. 65

Sir Charles Villiers Stanford
(1852–1924)

1908/9 No. 3 from *For Children*, Vol. 1

Béla Bartók
(1881–1945)

AB 2841

A collection of piano pieces, *For Children* was inspired by Slovakian or, as in this case, Hungarian folk music, which Bartók collected and recorded from 1906 onwards.

1923 Lullaby
from *Five Piano Pieces*

Frederick Delius
(1862–1934)

(The original metronome marking, for the piano piece, is ♩ = 44–48.)

© Copyright 1925 by Hawkes & Son (London) Ltd. Arranged and reproduced by permission of Boosey & Hawkes Music Publishers Ltd.

1940 Song at Dusk

from *Duets for Children*

William Walton
(1902–1983)

1940 Trumpet Tune

from *Duets for Children*

William Walton
(1902–1983)

AB 2841

1950 Simple Gifts

from *Old American Songs 1*

Shaker song arr.
Aaron Copland
(1900–1990)

2000 Hunt the Horn

Paul Harris

Printed in England by Caligraving Ltd, Thetford, Norfolk

Music origination by
Barnes Music Engraving Ltd, East Sussex

1950 Simple Gifts

from *Old American Songs 1*

Shaker song arr.
Aaron Copland
(1900–1990)

2000   Hunt the Horn

Paul Harris

Music origination by
Barnes Music Engraving Ltd, East Sussex

Printed in England by Caligraving Ltd, Thetford, Norfolk

AB 2841

02:10

The 'St Anthony' Variations by Brahms was based on a chorale attributed to Joseph Haydn. In fact the original chorale, scored for wind instruments, is probably not the work of Haydn.

1881 Agnus Dei

from *Messe basse*

Gabriel Fauré
(1845–1924)

1886 Wine Cellar

from *50 Russian Folksongs*

Pyotr Il'yich Tchaikovsky
(1840–1893)

AB 2841

1896   O Mistress Mine

from *The Clown's Songs from 'Twelfth Night'*, Op. 65

Sir Charles Villiers Stanford
(1852–1924)

1908/9 No. 3 from *For Children*, Vol. 1

Béla Bartók
(1881–1945)

A collection of piano pieces, *For Children* was inspired by Slovakian or, as in this case, Hungarian folk music, which Bartók collected and recorded from 1906 onwards.

1923 Lullaby

from *Five Piano Pieces*

Frederick Delius
(1862–1934)

(The original metronome marking, for the piano piece, is ♩ = 44–48.)

poco rit.   a tempo

dim. al fine

dim. al fine

morendo

pppp

1940 Song at Dusk

from *Duets for Children*

William Walton
(1902–1983)

1940 Trumpet Tune

from *Duets for Children*

William Walton
(1902–1983)

1950 Simple Gifts
from *Old American Songs 1*

Shaker song arr.
Aaron Copland
(1900–1990)

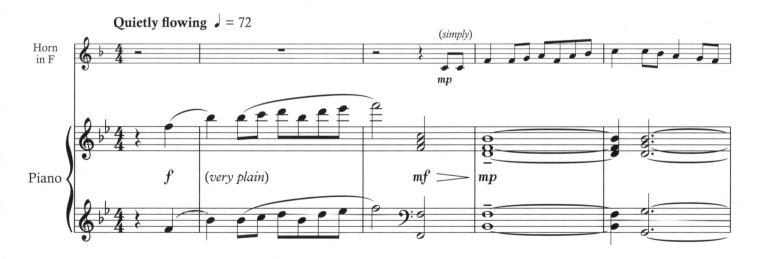

2000 Hunt the Horn

Paul Harris

Printed in England by Caligraving Ltd, Thetford, Norfolk

Music origination by
Barnes Music Engraving Ltd, East Sussex

AB 2841

02:10